First published in 2002 by
Franklin Watts
96 Leonard Street
London
EC2A 4XD

Franklin Watts Australia
56 O'Riordan Street
Alexandria
NSW 2015

A CIP catalogue record for this book is available
from the British Library.

ISBN 0 7496 4702 7 (hbk)
ISBN 0 7496 4709 4 (pbk)

Series Editor: Jackie Hamley
Series Advisor: Dr Barrie Wade
Cover Design: Jason Anscomb
Design: Peter Scoulding

Printed in Hong Kong

HOPSCOTCH

Whose Birthday Is It?

by Sherryl Clark and Jan Smith

W
FRANKLIN WATTS
LONDON•SYDNEY

It was a week until Luke's birthday.
He wanted to have a party but he
had just moved to a new school.

He hadn't made any friends yet.

"Let's have a birthday party in the park," said Mum and Dad. "There are lots of gardens to play in."

"I don't want a party," Luke replied. "No one will come." But his parents didn't listen.

"I'll dress up as a clown," said Dad, happily. "And do magic tricks."

"Yes, and I'll dress up as a fairy,"
added Mum. "I'll tell stories."

9

Mum and Dad helped Luke to write out party invitations for everyone in his class.

That night, Luke cut off "It's Luke's Birthday!" from the top of the invitations. All that was left was "Come to my party in the park!" and the date and time.

The next morning before class,
Luke put invitations on every
desk in his classroom.

He thought the other children
would throw them away.
But they didn't!

"I wonder whose party it is,"
said Raj, looking for a name.
"Maybe it's a pop star!" cried
Amy, excitedly.
"He wouldn't invite you then!"
teased Thomas.

Luke was amazed. Everyone wanted to go to the party! It was a big, exciting mystery.

On Saturday, Mum and Dad got all the food ready. Then Mum dressed up as a fairy and Dad dressed up as a clown.

They walked to the park, carrying
the food for the party. People
stared and smiled.

They laid out the food on a big tablecloth. Mum and Dad sat in the sun and waited.

Luke sneaked away and hid
behind some trees.

Then all the children from Luke's
class walked into the park.

"Welcome," said the clown.

He gave a balloon to each child.

"Lovely to see you!" said the fairy.

She gave out lollies and hats.

Soon everyone was playing games
and having a wonderful time.
They had forgotten it was
somebody's birthday.

They didn't know that the fairy
and the clown were Luke's
Mum and Dad.

Luke didn't want to hide any more.

He wanted to have fun, too.

He joined in a balloon game.

He helped to find the treasure in the treasure hunt. It was a box of chocolates wrapped in gold paper.

The fairy brought out the birthday cake. Everyone said: "This is a great party. Whose birthday is it?" "Don't you know?" said the clown. "It's Luke's birthday!"

They all cheered when Luke blew
out the candles on his cake.

Then they gave him his
birthday presents.

But the best present for Luke was
having so many new friends.

31

Hopscotch has been specially designed to fit the requirements of the National Literacy Strategy. It offers real books by top authors and illustrators for children developing their reading skills.

There are 12 Hopscotch stories to choose from:

Marvin, the Blue Pig
Written by Karen Wallace, illustrated by Lisa Williams

0 7496 4473 7 (hbk)
0 7496 4619 5 (pbk)

Plip and Plop
Written by Penny Dolan, illustrated by Lisa Smith

0 7496 4474 5 (hbk)
0 7496 4620 9 (pbk)

The Queen's Dragon
Written by Anne Cassidy, illustrated by Gwyneth Williamson

0 7496 4472 9 (hbk)
0 7496 4618 7 (pbk)

Flora McQuack
Written by Penny Dolan, illustrated by Kay Widdowson

0 7496 4475 3 (hbk)
0 7496 4621 7 (pbk)

Willie the Whale
Written by Joy Oades, illustrated by Barbara Vagnozzi

0 7496 4477 X (hbk)
0 7496 4623 3 (pbk)

Naughty Nancy
Written by Anne Cassidy, illustrated by Desideria Guicciardini

0 7496 4476 1 (hbk)
0 7496 4622 5 (pbk)

Run!
Written by Sue Ferraby, illustrated by Fabiano Fiorin

0 7496 4698 5 (hbk)
0 7496 4705 1 (pbk)

The Playground Snake
Written by Brian Moses, illustrated by David Mostyn

0 7496 4699 3 (hbk)
0 7496 4706 X (pbk)

"Sausages!"
Written by Anne Adeney, illustrated by Roger Fereday

0 7496 4700 0 (hbk)
0 7496 4707 8 (pbk)

The Truth about Hansel and Gretel
Written by Karina Law, illustrated by Elke Counsell

0 7496 4701 9 (hbk)
0 7496 4708 6 (pbk)

Pippin's Big Jump
Written by Hilary Robinson, illustrated by Sarah Warburton

0 7496 4703 5 (hbk)
0 7496 4710 8 (pbk)

Whose Birthday Is It?
Written by Sherryl Clark, illustrated by Jan Smith

0 7496 4702 7 (hbk)
0 7496 4709 4 (pbk)